I0518712

100 People Who Changed My World

by Ideas with Ink

No dreams were killed in the making of this book

Copyright © 2018 Ideas with Ink
All rights reserved.
101 Panya Publishing
101panya@gmail.com
ISBN- 1988880084
ISBN- 978-1-988880-08-2

To myself age 5

I miss you.

To myself age 25

Image not available yet

I look forward to meeting you.

I got rejected from my dream university and flunked the math exam yesterday. I woke up with crazy hair and in that moment, realized that I've done nothing meaningful with my life so far.

-diary entry from December 16, 2017

How about I make a movie?
Too expensive.

How about I audition for a play?
Suck at acting.

How about I write a book?
English teacher told me I was talentless. No, screw him, I'm going do it, ~~maybe~~, ~~someday~~, ~~possibly~~, today.

-diary entry from December 19, 2017

THE BAD PEOPLE

To my ex who cheated on me:

We met in chemistry class, and we had so much chemistry. You swept me off my feet, and I fell for you. I miss your laugh, blue hair and the wonderfully stupid poems you wrote for me. I miss the short walks in the park by your house, the long walks in the park by my house, and the person I was with you. I miss having someone to text when my day sucked and someone to call when my day rocked. One day out of the blue, you told me, "I can't be with you anymore" and I became blue. Later on, I found out from my friends that you had been playing me (now I get why love is called a game) and were dating another guy for months. We had history together the next semester, and we had so much history.

You're like a valley to me,  but

his mountain  , so be his mountain

and don't be anything for me. I found my Everest

and now I'm on top of the world.

To a rich guy who thinks he's better than anyone else:

You're like a country:

economically rich, morally poor.
So, are you truly rich or poor?

To somebody I dislike:

You're like a **wall.**

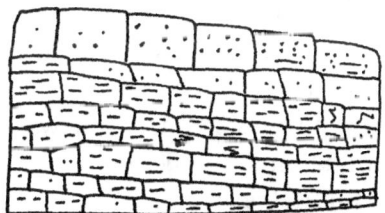

You terrify people.
You restrict people.
You unnerve people.
You marginalize people.
You punish people.

To a racist teacher:

In middle school, when I took your art class, you treated white students and students of colour differently. You tried to kill my dreams of becoming an artist, but, if your dreams are killed, they will be reborn as miracles.

To be honest, you put me in a box, a jam and a hole. I got out of the box, gobbled the jam and climbed out of the hole.

Screw you, I'm awesome.

You're like a factory because all you do is create problems, waste time, and pollute minds.

Firstly, you create problems. You create problems when you refuse to help me. You create problems when you call me inappropriate names.

Also, you waste time. You waste my time. I'm not learning anything being bullied by you and feeling uncomfortable.

Finally, you pollute minds. You pollute the minds of young people. Remember: every single mind you pollute is a mind that becomes sick.

In conclusion, you're like a factory, because all you do is create problems, waste time and pollute minds.

To a bully:

You're like a bomb  because you have an explosive temper, a short fuse, and you blow up.

To another bully: you're like a gun.

I needed a trigger warning before I met you.

To yet another bully:

You're like a missile. You tried to destroy my world.

To finally, yet, another bully:

You're like a knife because you stabbed me in the back and then cut me out of your life.

To the teacher who bullied a friend because of her sexuality:

My friend got up when the principal asked all queer and trans students to be recognized on national coming out day. She stood up, but all you cared about was that she stood out.

Later on, after class, you went on a rant and told her that homosexuality is unnatural.

Well, you know what, being a d*** is also unnatural.

You're like an arrow ⟫⟫⟶▷ because you're straight and narrow, and because you can hurt people.

To the teacher who sexually harassed my friend:

My friend and I were students in your biology class. While we were studying predators in the ecosystem, little did I know that there was a predator in our midst.

You stared at her with your stupid blue eyes. You hit on her with your stupid voice. You told her one day you guys would be living happily ever after, but, let's be real, fairy tales are fake.

One day, another teacher saw and heard you guys together after school talking about tying the knot and reported it.

You made up some bs, blamed my friend, and got away with it.

You broke her so much, that her heart shattered. You destroyed her so much so, that her head was in the clouds thinking, if it was time to move to heaven.

You're like a clock.
#time's up because what you're doing is alarming.

To this racist kid who made fun of me:

We are on a school trip camping in a beautiful forest (not sure what it's called).
All of a sudden, this kid who constantly bullies me shouted, "You know what you have in common with a bear?!"
I replied, "What?"
He exclaimed, "You're fat, brown and an animal."
I don't want to write anything else for now because I'm sad.

- diary entry from May 13, 2015

You're like a zoo because you told me I was an animal.

Then, I learned in biology that humans were animals too.

So, we all are animals after all.

To this other racist kid who made fun of me:

I brought brownies to class for my birthday one year, and you said, "Thanks for the brownie, brownie."
Then you corrected yourself and exclaimed, "No, actually, you're a coconut because you're brown on the outside, but white on the inside."

You're like a grocery store because you called me a coconut, but I have the last laugh because coconuts are out of season, and, I hope, when you go vacationing in the  Maldives and sit under a palm tree on a beach a coconut falls right next to you and kills your ego.

Oh, wait, your ego would probably just be injured because it's so

BIG.

To this older kid who hazed younger students like me in high school and who, I discovered, got hazed when he went to college:

I was like a little fish.

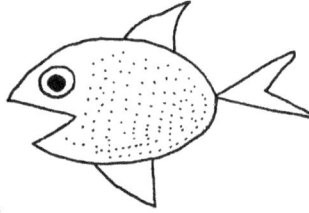

You were like a big fish.

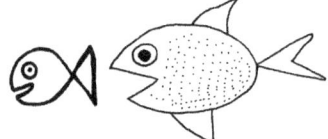

You tried to eat me.

 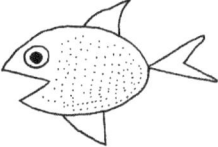

I swam away.

An even bigger fish ate you.

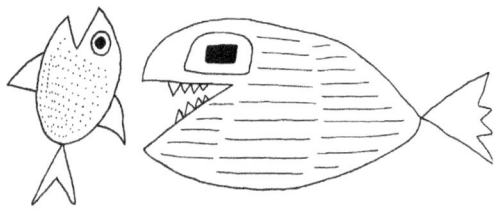

To this rich kid who brags about how famous his dad is:

You're like a bird.

    The only reason you can fly is because you were born with wings. Remember that.

    Not everybody has wings. Not everybody can fly.

can fly.   can't fly.

To this person who I met online and started cyber dating before I realized that the profile was fake:

You're like a unicorn because you're not real.
You're too beautiful to be real.
You're too rich to be real.
You're too good to be real.
You had a killer sense of humor, so I died of laughter, and now I have to leave fantasyland and go back to Earth to be resuscitated.
Bye for now, my unicorn.

To this rich, straight, white dude who pretends he's a person of colour and that he too experiences racism:

You're like a vulture because you steal our cultures, struggles and identities.

The world is your oyster.

Why do you have to steal the scraps that we get?

THE OK PEOPLE

To the teacher who made fun of me for being molested:

During the winter of my life, I went to you after class and broke down.
I opened myself up to you about being a survivor, but you were close-minded and said: "You're a guy, why didn't you defend yourself?".
I wish, I said something smart like, "Anybody can be a victim and a survivor", but I was stunned and walked out.
You were so cold, but, hey, that's winter in Canada for you. My winter lasted for two more years, but now I'm in the spring of my life, and alive, and you're still cold.

You're like a box because you

```
think inside the box.
```

Men can be victims too.

To the teacher who told my friend to take off her hijab because it was against the dress code:

You're like a washing machine

because
you wash all of our colors off
and everybody
becomes

the same *boring* grey,

so, please, stop.

To a teacher who believes
discrimination doesn't exist:

You're like a fridge.

You want me to eat b*llsh*t
but I'm hungry for change.
I'm starving for justice.
I'm famished for equality.
I'm craving peace.

To somebody I went on a blind date with:

I went on my first blind date with someone my friend set me up with. We met at Starbucks, the one near (my/our) school. My date tells me right away: "This isn't going to be love at first sight." (I'm not skinny, but, honestly, how rude). I respond, "Isn't love blind?"

Then, after like three minutes of awkward silence, all of a sudden, my date asks me if I want to go to back to their place to have a cup of coffee.
*I said: "We're at Starbucks, dumb***."*
My date storms out and I order a drink with six pumps of raspberry syrup, coconut, coffee, and a bunch of caramel and realize that being single is awesome.

I realized three things today:
  1. *A cup of coffee probably means more.*
  2. *You lose your virginity when you give a f*** about someone else.*
  3. *Stick to the menu options at Starbucks.*

-diary entry from June 28, 2017

You're like a pair of glasses because you made me see that love is not blind.
She must have x-ray vision
 because she saw that you didn't have a heart.

To a classmate who made fun of my PTSD after I got molested, but then actually realized that it was a real thing when he got diagnosed with PTSD after his friend died in a car accident that he was a part of:

You're like a pair of shoes.

You used to walk all over me, but then you walked a mile in my shoes and realized, that my shoes are worn out from going up mountains and down valleys, non-stop.

To my classmate who offered me weed and alcohol:

At a house party, you offered me a beer, and I drank it.

At a house party, you offered me pot, and I smoked it.

I was hammered, but my friend was tougher than nails and drove me home.

I was stoned, but my friend was my rock and drove me home.

You're like a pill because

you make me forget my past

by ignoring my present

and screwing up my future.

To the person who broke up with me:

We met at summer camp, were together for all of July, and my heart was on fire in the heat of the summer. Then, you texted me on the last day of camp:

I'm breaking up with you because I don't love who I am around you.

(And I just started crying, and my tears extinguished the fire in my heart.)

You're like a hammer

because it was you who broke my heart

(but my heart got up and put itself back together).

To a celebrity of colour who makes me feel comfortable and valued with being brown:

You're like a mirror because I can see myself in you. Thanks for helping me feel OK with the way I talk, the way I walk, and the way I live. Thanks for making me feel comfortable in my own skin, *literally*.

When I turn on the TV and see someone who resembles me, it makes me feel that hard work "trumps" discrimination.

To the teacher who let me join her club when all the other clubs I applied to rejected me:

You're like a door because you were open-minded and gave me a chance when I needed it most, and nobody else would help.

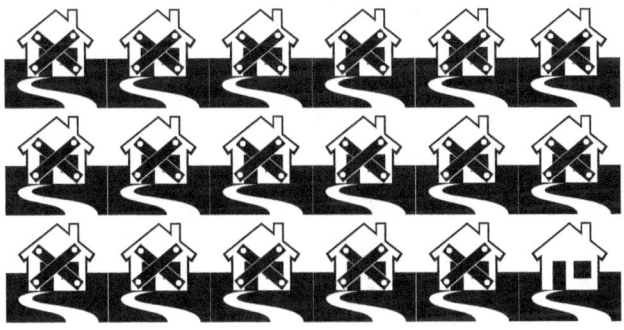

Rejection creates opportunities.

To my classmate who refuses to acknowledge that privilege exists:

You're like a bed. You want me to fall asleep, but I need to stay woke. I need to stay woke because people of colour are getting killed by the cops every day because of their **race**. I need to stay woke because women are getting assaulted and killed by their partners because of their **sex**. I need to stay woke because queer and trans people are killing themselves because people can't accept them for their **sexuality and gender**. I need to stay woke because people with disabilities are getting abandoned and killed by their parents because of their **disability**. I need to stay woke because Muslims are getting assaulted and killed by strangers for wearing hijabs, kufis, and burqas because of their **religion**. I need to stay woke because low-income people are getting sick and dying because they don't have access to healthcare or clean water because of their **class**. I need to stay woke, because kids like me are getting up, leaving their homes, walking to school and getting shot there. RIP. I need to stay woke because every person who turns a blind eye to problems is as good as dead and **I'm still alive**.

To a waiter who made fun of my mom's Russian accent, pretended not to understand her (but later apologized):

To someone I went on a blind date with and who thinks that racial colorblindness is acceptable:

You're like a TV.

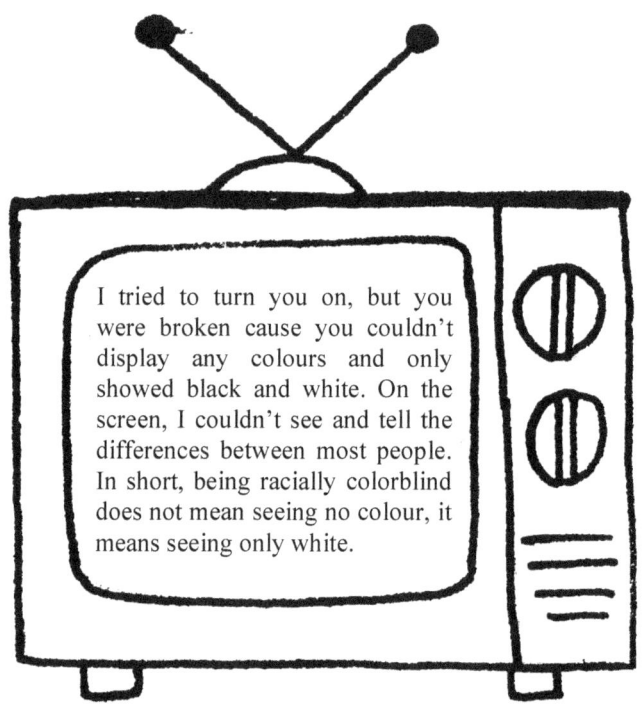

To my friend who decided to drop out of school and
spends the days getting high:

You're like a toilet.
Stop hanging around shi*** people.
(And make the Dic*hea** pis* off
and the As*h**** give a shi* about you.)

To my friend who decided to drop out of school and
spends the day getting drunk:

You're like a garbage can.
Stop hanging around trashy people
and   throw   them   out   of   your   life.

To my ex crush in who I lost all interest after I realized all they wanted from me was to buy them things:

You're like a shovel ⟨▭━━━▭⟩. I used to have a

heart of gold. I was digging you, but you were

actually digging my heart because you were a gold

digger. You kept mining my heart till you left me in

a   deep   hole,   and   you   became   an

imaginary millionaire.

To a person who I dated and who only cared about themselves:

You're like a hole.

I was

falling

for you.

for me.

I'm climbing

Now

33

To my friend

who studies

and works:

You're like a nail.

To my friend

who takes drugs

and parties:

You're like a screw.

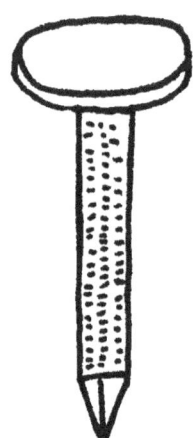

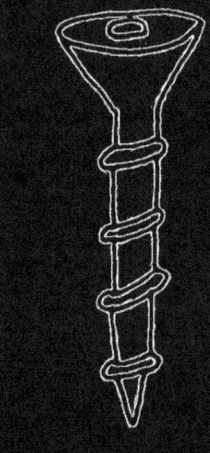

You're nailing life.

You're screwing up life.

To this smart girl who studied so hard in high
school, went to great university, then got with the
wrong crowd, and eventually dropped up:

You're like a candle:
your future was so bright
until you burned out,
and
I don't know what else to say,
except,
I
hope,
that

you catch *fire* again.

To my friend who wants to be a comedian, is hilarious and breaks the stereotype that women can't be funny:

You're like a lamp because you're so lit, and because you have so many lightbulb moments, and because you light up the room, and because your future is bright, and because you light up my life.

To this guy who got into a great university and is a great student:

You're like a gold medal because you're winning at life.

To this guy who got into a good university and is a good student:

You're like a silver medal because you're sort of winning at life.

To this guy who got into an okay university and is an okay student:

You're like a bronze medal because you're doing okay at life, but, hey, at least you're happier than the silver medal guy, because success and happiness aren't synonyms, and because in this screwed up world being average is better than being **almost** extraordinary.

To a classmate who was homeless for many years and had to sleep in a laundromat before her and her mom could afford a place to call home:

Congrats on getting into a university and I honestly wish you all the best.

You're like a boxing glove because you're constantly fighting. You've tripped over the poverty line, hit your head on the   glass ceiling, got locked in the closet, and it is inspiring that you're still standing up ready to fight the world.

To the girl at our school who became the first woman of colour to be elected as student body president:

You're like an axe because you shattered the glass ceiling. You didn't just break it, cause women of colour shatter the glass ceiling, they don't just break it.

To someone who I judged based on the way he talked and then realized what he talked about was brilliant:

You're like a book.

Thanks for teaching me to judge a book by its message, not cover, not title, not size, not setting, not price.

To a kid at summer camp whose counsellor I was:
You were non-verbal and, yet, you taught me the value of words and the importance of having a voice.

You're like a microphone.
You never spoke and, yet, you spoke the loudest because you reminded me not to be scared of my voice.

To a psychologist my mom took me to:

Thank you for teaching me techniques to help alleviate my mental issues and control my anxiety.

You're like a pair of headphones because you helped me mute the voices in my head.

To the girl who was the head of the school newspaper and who published my very first poem:

Thanks, from the bottom of my heart and also the top of my heart.

You're like a fan because you're my fan.

Thank you for publishing my work :)

To an indigenous girl who went missing many moons ago, at the same age as I am now:

Across Canada, hundreds of Indigenous women have gone missing and been murdered. Lack of care by law enforcement has resulted in only few of these cases being solved.

You're missing and badly needed.

−   like a puzzle piece that can't be found

To my classmate who came out as non-binary:

You're like a rubber duck

because

gender, unfortunately,

is like choosing

between being

a doll and a **toy soldier.**

And you were like, "Screw it!

I'm going to be a rubber duck."

To one of my best friends who laughs at my cheesy jokes (even if he's lactose intolerant):

You're a gift

because you're gifting me with your presence.

You're like a present

because you make my present enjoyable.

To a classmate who comes from a difficult background with a single mom and lives in government housing, but is determined to make something of himself:

You're like a car.

You have so much drive. You have so much drive.
You have so much drive. You have so much drive.
You have so much drive. You have so much drive.
You have so much drive. You have so much drive.
You have so much drive. You have so much drive.
You have so much drive. You have so much drive.
You have so much drive. You have so much drive.
You have so much drive. You're going places.

To my friend who I thought loved me, but abandoned me when I was depressed, and started bullying me:

You're like a train.

My mom said, "Real friends stay during the tough times."

When my life got derailed,

you left me faster than a high-speed train,

and now you're heading towards Hell.

STOP while you can.

To a nice person, I never had the courage to talk to:

You had orange hair, and dimples, and wore a jean jacket, and were smart and kind, and I was shy.

You're like a road.   I'm like a road.

Our paths never crossed.

To a classmate who has opposing political views:

I can sympathize with you, but I can't empathize with you.

You're like a rocket ship,

but understanding other people is rocket science, and I'm not a rocket scientist.

To this girl with who I used to be friends with:

We grew up. We grew apart.

You're like a boat.

It was smooth sailing
until I rocked the boat,
fell into the ocean of tears (depression),
nearly drowned (suicide attempt),
swam alone for a while (loneliness),
and found a school of fish (new friends).

The Good People

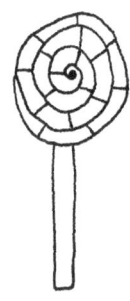

To my best friend forever:

I wanted to kill myself, and you helped me
overcome my hatred of myself by loving me:

You're like a farm.

When it was raining tears,

I decided to plant kisses.

And that's

how our love greW.

To a rich but hardworking guy:

You're like a cake.

 You were made from the best eggs, and milk, and sugar, and flour, and that's why life is such a piece of cake for you. You've realized and acknowledged that and I appreciate that.

To my family friend who started his business with nothing and kept working hard, and smart, and is incredibly successful:

You're like a loaf of bread.

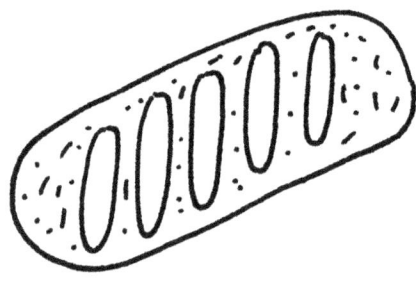

You're made of dough, because you rose above it all.

To a stranger who came from a war-torn country:

We met while taking the SAT because you forgot your ID and had to use my phone to call your mom to bring it.

After the test that I bombed, you casually told me about how you left your country because of bombings. You talked about the war in your country, and the terror, and fear, and the hope, and the plane ride to get here.

I remember just being stunned and thinking how lucky I was to be born in Canada.

You're a tough cookie	because you didn't crumble
or crack,	or break,
or burn,	in the oven called life.

To a nice person
who life screwed
over:

You're like a lemon
because you're so
sour.

To a nice person
who life really
screwed over:

You're like a pretzel,
because you're so
salty.

To a nice person
who life f*****
over:

You're like a cup of
coffee, because
you're so bitter.

To a nice person who
life really f*****
over, but who is so
resilient:

You're like a
lollipop, because
you're so sweet.

To a nice person with who I can't get along with:

You're like
a cup of tea,
 just not
my cup of
tea .

To a classmate who gets bullied because of his mental illness:

You are an ~~nut~~ anything you want to be.

To a classmate who gets bullied because of his religion:

You are an ~~kebab~~ anything you want to be.

To a classmate who gets bullied because of his sexuality:

You are an ~~fruitcake~~ anything you want to be.

To a classmate who gets bullied because of his skin color:

You are an ~~coconut~~ anything you want to be.

I'm not gonna define you guys :)

To a kid who had anorexia:

I met you in the hospital while getting help for my PTSD.

You're like a plate.

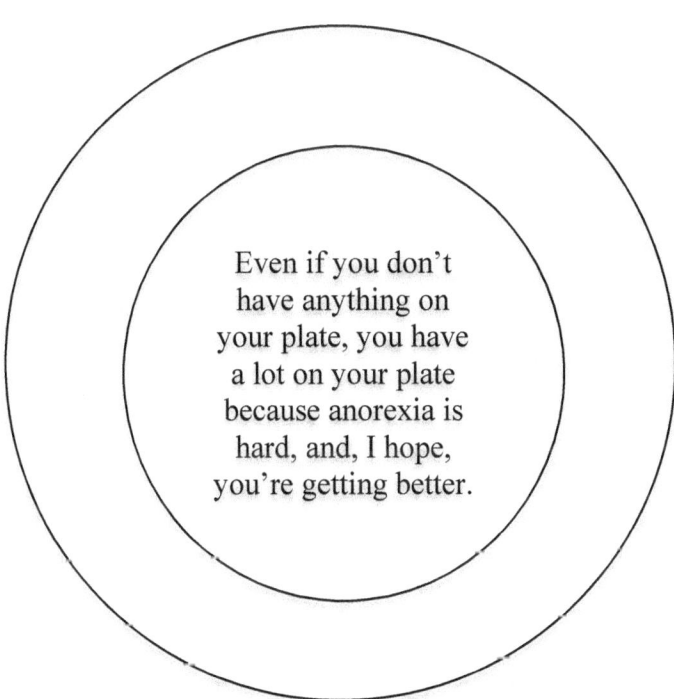

Even if you don't have anything on your plate, you have a lot on your plate because anorexia is hard, and, I hope, you're getting better.

To a classmate who's black:

People call you dark chocolate.

To a classmate who's brown:

People call you milk chocolate.

To a classmate who's white:

People call you white chocolate,

but all of you are, honestly, just beautiful no matter the colour of your skin because you're all amazing people.

Let's make this the year when *who* we are is more important than *what* we are.

To a friend who tutors me in partying:

You're like a piece of candy.

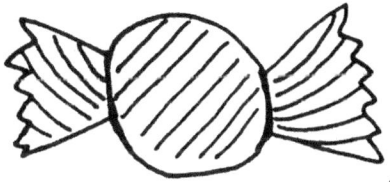

I want you.

To a friend who tutors me in math:

You're like a salad.

I need you.

To this girl who survived being r**** by another student at my school:

You're like a rose. You survived the rain, the storm, the lighting, the thunder, the cold, and the world is in love with you.

Beauty can grow from pain,

and you're like a beautiful flower.

To my cousin who helped me when I was
depressed:

You're like a cactus.

My heart used to be a forest.

When the animals left me - you stayed.

When the trees left me - you stayed.

When the flowers left me - you stayed.

When my heart became a desert -

You were the only thing

Still alive in my heart.

To a teenager who was 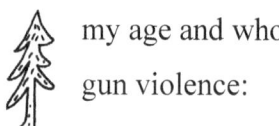 my age and who was killed because of gun violence:

You're like a tree.

You were a tiny seed, but still, you grew.

You had less water and sunlight than other trees, but still, you grew.

You were called ugly by the other trees, but still, you grew.

Some guy chopped you down because he didn't like that you were dark green when all the other trees were light green.

You never had the chance to grow roots.

You never had the chance to grow fruit.

You never had the chance to grow up, to be a big, beautiful tree that people go on Sundays and picnic under, or where little kids play hide and seek, or where two awkward teenagers have their first kiss.

It's not fair that I'm still alive and you're **not**.

To my friend who is getting better after being diagnosed with depression:

You're were a desert of emptiness.

Now you're a rainforest full of life.

To my aunt who loves me unconditionally:

You're like a university.

Thanks for accepting me.

To my uncle:

You're like a school.

You taught me:

Respect, honesty, integrity, hope, love, peace.

To my frenemy:
you're like a pencil.

I erased you from my memory.

To my friend:
You're like a pen.

I couldn't erase you from my memory.

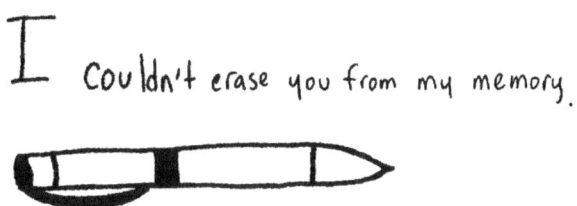

To my best friend:
You're like an eraser. You helped me erase my
(bad) memories.

To my grade 9 math teacher:

You taught how to find y and also why.

You're like a sharpener.

I was dull. You made me **sharp**.

To a friend who made me realize that my significant other was not good:

You're like a ruler.

You helped me draw the line.

To my great-grandpa who died from cancer:

You're like a calculator:

because you told me that,

"Even, though, my days are numbered

my love for you is infinite,"

And then you died a week later.

To my grandma:

You're like a microscope.

You told me, "Don't overlook the small things."

To my other grandma:

You're like a telescope.

You told me, "Don't forget the big picture."

To a girl of colour who presented a speech on her experiences with sexism and racism at our school:

You're like a camera
because you showed
your lens,
your tragically
beautiful lens,
on this world.
When I see a street,
you see a battlefield.

When I see a nightclub, you see a warzone.
When I see the world, you see a bomb.
And that's just unfair.
Even in times of peace,
women of colour are battling racism and sexism
everywhere.

To my childhood friend who moved to another country and with who I no longer keep in contact with:

You're like a museum because we have so much history:

All of our fights, discoveries, inventions.

But history is in the past.
And you're in my past.
And I'm in your past.

To the kid who I framed:

In first grade, someone brought cupcakes, and I took the caramel one without asking. In panic, I gobbled the cupcake and left the wrapper in your cubby. The kid whose birthday it was noticed that the cupcake he wanted was gone and started bawling. The teacher found the wrapper in your cubby, so you got in trouble.

Years later we met up, and I told you about this incident for some random reason, and we laughed, and, by the way, you have turned into such a great person.

You're like a painting.

I framed you.

Sorry :(

To my friend who self-harms:

You're a gem.

You're a gem in a world of shi*** people.

Remember, nothing* can cut you, because you're a diamond.

* nothing, except yourself.

To a friend who is insecure with their body:
You are so beautiful :).

You're like a place of worship.

Your body is a temple.

All you need to do is believe in yourself.

Your body is a church.

All you need to do is believe in yourself.

Your body is a mosque.

All you need to do is believe in yourself.

Your body is a shrine.

All you need to do is believe in yourself.

Your body is a synagogue.

All you need to do is believe in yourself.

To this person who I had a fling with:

You're like a jail.

I'm in here for stealing your heart,

and it was worth it.

The guy next to me is in here for killing your time.

The girl next to me is in here for stealing your peace of mind.

I'm the *least* guilty.

To my counsellor,

You're like a hospital  because you saved me.

When my heart was broken,

you stitched it back together.

When my mind was cloudy,

you cleared it up.

To myself.

I'm like an eye:

But I'm also an
I:

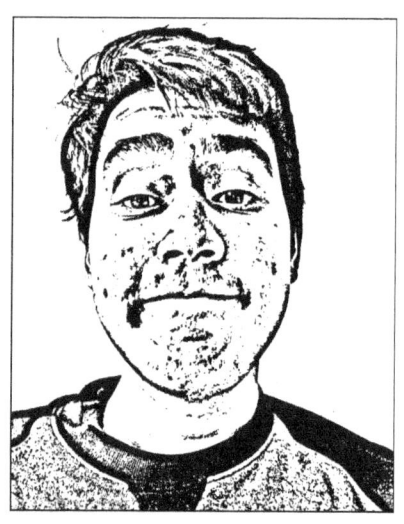

To my friend who's a model, but gets constantly
Photoshopped:

You're like a heart.

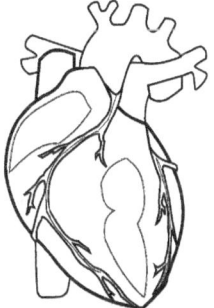

This is you:

Powerful, smart, kind.

But society wants

you to be this:

Something that doesn't exist.

And that's screwed up.

To the class genius or the class idiot:

You say the most amazing things that are so random and weird, so I can't tell if you're a genius or an idiot.

You're like a brain.
Here is your coolest or stupidest thought:

"Kids are aliens because no one gets them;

And adults are robots because all they do is work;

And seniors are ghosts because they're invisible to others".

To a classmate who moved from a different country and feels inadequate
compared to other kids at school:

You think you're an alien.
"Immigrant are like aliens," you told me, "They come from a different planet."

But remember, whether you're Afghan or Albanian or Algerian or American
or Andorran or Angolan or Antiguans or Argentinean or Armenian or
Australian or Austrian or Azerbaijani or Bahamian or Bahraini or Bangladeshi
or Barbadian or Barbudan or Bissau-Guinean or Botswanan or Belarusian or
Belgian or Belizean or Beninese or Bhutanese or Bolivian or Bosnian or
Botswanan or Brazilian or Basotho or British or Bruneian or Bulgarian or
Burkinabe or Burmese or Burundian or Cambodian or Cameroonian or
Canadian or Cape Verdean or Central African or Chadian or Chilean or
Chinese or Colombian or Comorian or Congolese or Costa Rican or Croatian
or Cuban or Cypriot or Czech or Danish or Djiboutian or Dominican or Dutch
or Ecuadorean or Egyptian or Emirati or Equatorial Guinean or Eritrean or
Estonian or Ethiopian or Fijian or Filipino or Finnish or French or Gabonese
or Gambian or Georgian or German or Ghanaian or Greek or Grenadian or
Guatemalan or Guinean or Guyanese or Haitian or Herzegovinian or
Honduran or Hungarian or Icelander or I-Kiribati or Indian or Indonesian or
Iranian or Iraqi or Irish or Israeli or Italian or Ivorian or Jamaican or Japanese
or Jordanian or Kazakhstani or Kenyan or Kittian and Nevisian or Kosovan or
Kuwaiti or Kyrgyz or Laotian or Latvian or Lebanese or Liberian or Libyan or
Liechtensteiner or Lithuanian or Luxembourger or Macedonian or Malagasy
or Malawian or Malaysian or Maldivian or Malian or Maltese or Marshallese
or Mauritanian or Mauritian or Mexican or Micronesian or Moldovan or
Monacan or Mongolian or Moroccan or Mozambican or Namibian or Nauruan
or Nepalese or New Zealander or Nicaraguan or Nigerian or Nigerian or North
Korean or Northern Irish or Norwegian or Omani or Pakistani or Palauan or
Panamanian or Papua New Guinean or Paraguayan or Peruvian or Polish or
Portuguese or Qatari or Romanian or Russian or Rwandan or Saint Lucian or
Saint Vincentian or Salvadoran or Samoan or Sammarinese or Sao Tomean or
Saudi Arabian or Scottish or Senegalese or Serbian or Seychellois or Sierra
Leonean or Singaporean or Slovakian or Slovenian or Solomon Islander or
Somali or South African or South Korean or South Sudanese or Spanish or Sri
Lankan or Sudanese or Surinamer or Swazi or Swedish or Swiss or Syrian or
Taiwanese or Tajik or Tanzanian or Thai or Timorese or Togolese or Tongan
or Trinidadian or Tobagonian or Tunisian or Turkish or Turkmen or Tuvaluan
or Ugandan or Ukrainian or Uruguayan or Uzbek or Vatican or Vanuatuan or
Venezuelan or Vietnamese or Welsh or Yemeni or Zambian or Zimbabwean,

we all are from Earth.

To my friend who can't express his emotions because of society's expectations on how men should behave:

You're like a robot:

"Men are robots," you told me, "They can't show emotions."

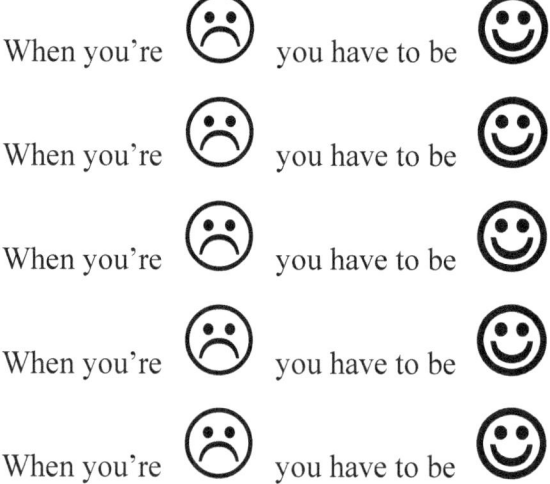

Cry, my friend. It's *okay.*

Anybody who acts okay when they're not deserves an Oscar

To my queer friend who can't show who she loves
because of heterosexism:

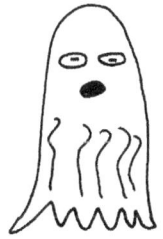

You're like a ghost:

"Queer people are ghosts," you told me, "They have
to hide their feelings."

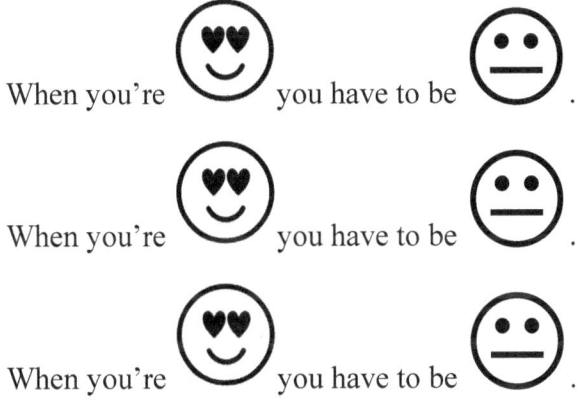

When you're ⊙ you have to be ⊙ .

When you're ⊙ you have to be ⊙ .

When you're ⊙ you have to be ⊙ .

It's *not your fault* that teenagers can be devils.

It's *not your fault* that high school is hell.

To a neighbour:
You're like a dinosaur

because you live in the PAST.

To another neighbour:
You're like a cyborg

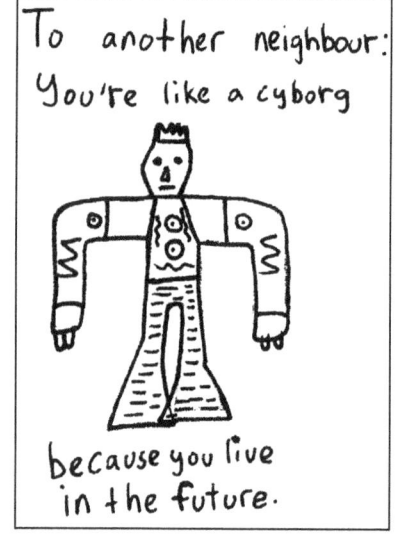

because you live
in the future.

To this boy who I followed on social media and who killed himself: RIP.

at age 13: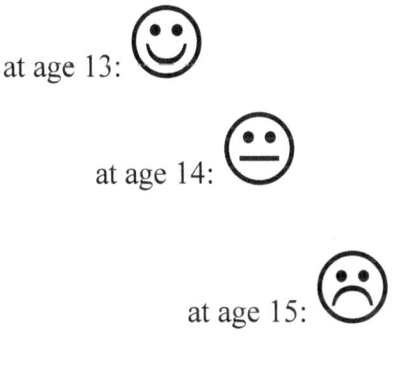

at age 14:

at age 15:

at age 16:

Now: **?**

Hopefully, an *angel*.

To anybody thinking about suicide, it's not worth it. You have a whole crazy life to live, no matter who you are. This is coming from experience and no, it's not worth it.

To my older sister:

You're like the .

I look up to you.

To my younger sister:

You're like a bridge

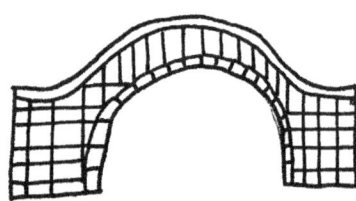

Because you bring our family closer together.

To my dad:

You're like a crane.

I'm like a skyscraper.

Thanks for giving me a solid foundation and building me up.

To a friend who's dead:

You were like a city: influential and full of
excitement.

One day, the ocean was hungry and swallowed you
whole.

To someone who I had a great relationship and still am friends with after breaking up:

You're like a castle.

Thanks for treating me like a king. :)

To my significant other:

You're like a mountain to me because you're my

high point in life. I found my Everest, and now I'm

on top of the world.

To my great grandma:
You're my gun book plane car
train rocketship boat pencil pen
bomb phone tv stone paper
bullet (ROCK) tree fire ice
newspaper tiger crocodile zebra
xylophone piano saxophone deer
violin globe map gem toilet
oven toaster pan pot wrench

To my mom:

You are ~~a~~ my ~~house~~ ~~house~~ ~~house~~
~~house~~ ~~house~~ ~~house~~ ~~house~~ ~~house~~
~~house~~ ~~house~~ ~~house~~ ~~house~~ ~~house~~
~~house~~ ~~house~~ (HOME) ~~house~~ ~~house~~
~~house~~ ~~house~~ ~~house~~ ~~house~~ ~~house~~
~~house~~ ~~house~~ ~~house~~ ~~house~~ ~~house~~

To this kid in my class who is a great poet:

Last week you said, "Everybody will have a Mount Everest and a Death Valley moment in their life."

And I was likc, "So truc."

You're like the ocean

Because you're so deep.

To my friend struggling with depression:

You're like the sky
because you're blue
and because your
mind is cloudy.

Remember, every
single tear you cry
was probably
dinosaur piss, or
caveman spit, or
gladiator tears.

To my friend, who wants to save the planet:

You constantly remind to turn off the lights and pick up trash. You convinced me to go vegan, which I did. I was shocked when you said "**If earth was our kid, then we'd be in jail for child abuse**".

You're like a forest because you're so green.

To the woman at the suicide hotline who talked me out of killing myself:

Thanks for telling me I was beautiful, and smart, and kind, and worth it, and that life was precious, and that the dark times would pass.

You're like the sun.

Without you, I wouldn't be alive because my world needs to the sun to survive.

Without you, there would be one less person laughing and smiling on this planet.

But with you, there is one more person laughing and smiling on this planet.

I'm laughing and smiling as I write this.

To a classmate who became famous:

In a world of snowflakes

be a star

and a star you have become.

To myself part 2:

I'm a planet
        because
                I'm my own world.

And finally:

A petition from me to you:

Let's stop treating each other like crap.

1.

2. _____

Sources:

Thanks to my parents, sister and dog for supporting me.

Black Cartoon Heart image is from
https://commons.wikimedia.org/wiki/File:Love_Heart_SVG.s
vg ©Bubinator

Human Heart image is from
https://pixabay.com/en/anatomical-healthcare-heart-human-
2023188/ ©Pixabay

Vulture image is from https://pixabay.com/en/vulture-brown-
big-beak-sit-animal-306727/ ©Pixabay

Cartoon eraser is from https://pixabay.com/en/eraser-rubber-
green-undo-office-307518/ ©Pixabay

Emojis are from ©Emojidex emoji
©emojidex https://www.emojidex.com and ©Twitter
(©Twemojis)

Heart Emoticon is from https://pixabay.com/en/emoji-
emoticon-icon-love-heart-1971631/ ©Pixabay by Tumisu

Wave Image is from https://pixabay.com/en/wave-big-foam-
ocean-power-blue-305226/ ©Pixabay

Fridge image is from https://pixabay.com/en/refrigerator-
frozen-refrigeration-1129919/ ©Pixabay by JJuni

About the Author:

Ideas with Ink is the pen name of a young author from Canada. I like walking in the rain, skies full of stars, ghost towns, my family, rainbows, writing, puppies, kittens, the way people come together in difficult times, camping, nice strangers and that the world is slowly but surely becoming a better place.

Please check out my first poetry book "Time Capsule", the poetic novel, "Nothing" and the children's books "The Dragon in the Glass Ball", "The Russian Journal" from the Fairytale Travel Series", and from The Tiger Family Stories: "Why Am I Vegetarian?". I am really happy and grateful that you read this book.

Note: You can contact me by e-mail at ideaswithink@gmail.com and please feel free to follow me on IG, FB, and Tw @ideaswithink

www.ingramcontent.com/pod-product-compliance
Lightning Source LLC
Chambersburg PA
CBHW070640130626
46555CB00006B/2634